The Dragon's Pearl

Retold by Julie Lawson
Paintings by Paul Morin

Clarion Books
New York

Lawson, Julie.

The dragon's pearl / by Julie Lawson : illustrated by Paul Morin.
p. cm
Summary: During a terrible drought, a cheerful, dutiful son finds
a magic pearl which forever changes his life and the lives of his
mother and neighbors.
ISBN 0-395-63623-X

[1. Pearls — Fiction.   2. Dragons — Fiction.   3. China — Fiction.
4. Fairy tales.]   I. Morin, Paul, 1959-   ill.   II. Title.
PZ8.L439Dr   1992
[Fic] — dc20

92-2574
CIP
AC

Clarion Books
a Houghton Mifflin Company imprint
215 Park Avenue South, New York, NY 10003
Text copyright © 1993 by Julie Lawson
Illustrations copyright © 1993 by Paul Morin
First published in Canada by Oxford University Press Canada,
70 Wynford Drive, Don Mills, Ontario M3C 1J9

Book design: Paul Morin
Photography by: Gary Freeman
All rights reserved.

**For information about permission to reproduce selections from
this book, write to Permissions,
Houghton Mifflin Company, 2 Park Street, Boston, MA 02108**

Printed in Hong Kong

To my good friend, Julie Cross.
With special thanks to Kathryn Cole
for her encouragement and support.

—J.L.

To Joseph Campbell who gave me the confidence
to follow my bliss,
and to magic moments in Yangshuo, China

—P.M.

In the faraway days of cloud-breathing dragons, there lived a boy named Xiao Sheng who loved to sing.

Not that he had much to sing about. He toiled from dawn till dusk cutting grass and selling it for fuel or fodder. In that way, he was able to earn just enough money to buy food for himself and his mother.

Still, Xiao Sheng was a good-natured boy.

"Good-bye, Mama," he said each day. "Who knows what the gods have in store for us. Today may not be the same as yesterday."

But each day was the same. Off Xiao Sheng would go, thinking how lovely the river looked in the early morning sun. He wished he could fish from its banks or swim in its cool water, but there was never time. With only his song for company, he cut the grass and carried it to the village to sell. At sunset, he made his way home for a bowl of rice, a cup of tea, and a welcome sleep. And each day was the same.

Then came a terrible drought. Day after day the sun beat upon the land. Streams no longer sparkled in the hills. The river burned like fire along its scorched banks.

As always Xiao Sheng sang to lift his spirits, but he was worried. He scanned the sky for a sign of the rain-bringing dragons, but there was never a trace, not even the silkiest wisp of a cloud. Farther and farther into the hills he went, searching for grass that was not shriveled and dead.

One day, as he reached the crest of the highest hill, Xiao Sheng gazed upon a splendid patch of rich, green grass. Eagerly he cut the whole patch and hurried to the village, where he sold it for more money than he had ever received before.

When he returned the next day, he discovered the grass had grown back.

"Thank you!" he said, bowing to whatever gods were responsible for his good fortune. Once again he cut the grass and rushed off to the village.

The same thing happened on the third day and on the fourth. Each morning the grass that had been cut had grown back as green and lush as ever.

An idea came to Xiao Sheng. "This must be magic grass," he said. "And if it grows so well here, why not anywhere? I'll plant it at home and save myself a long journey each day."

Next morning he began to dig up the grass, carefully moving the earth and roots to the tiny plot of land beside his hut.

Back and forth he went, digging and transplanting one small bit at a time. He was almost finished when he noticed something shimmering, deep in the earth. He reached for it— and gasped. For in his hand, glowing like a rose-colored sunset, lay a pearl.

He raced home, crying for joy. "Mama! See what the gods have given us!"

His old mother beamed. "This pearl will bring us a fortune. But let's keep it for a while before we lose sight of its beauty."

Xiao Sheng agreed, and he watched his mother hide the pearl in their near-empty rice jar. Then he went back to his planting.

"How wonderful it will be," he said. "Tomorrow I'll cut the grass right here. Maybe I'll have time to catch a fish for supper."

But it was not to be. Early next morning, Xiao Sheng rushed outside—
only to find that his grass had withered and died.

"What have I done!" he cried. And he cursed himself for disturbing
the earth, for destroying the rich, green grass, for being too happy and
tempting the gods.

In the midst of his tears a thought struck him.

"Perhaps I should have planted the pearl," he said. And he dashed off to the rice jar.

What a sight met his eyes! The jar was now brimming with rice, and on top of the rice lay the gleaming pearl.

"A magic pearl!" his mother exclaimed. "Let's put it in our money box and see what happens."

They placed the pearl beside the one coin in the money box, and in no time the box was brimful of gold.

"Ah!" the old woman gasped, running her fingers through the coins. "You were right, my son. Today is not the same as yesterday!"

How they rejoiced! Their oil jar overflowed, their rice jar was never empty, and their money box was always full. While their neighbors prayed for rain, Xiao Sheng and his mother sang for joy and blessed their precious pearl.

Their friends were not blind to their good fortune. Day after day they saw Xiao Sheng playing in the village or dreaming by the river. He brought home fish and no longer went into the hills to cut grass. He had always been a happy boy... but now!

"Have you ever seen such a smile?" the villagers said. "And how well his old mother looks! Surely the gods have favored these two."

The villagers were not angry or jealous, because wealth did not make Xiao Sheng and his mother selfish. They gave generously to everyone who had shown them kindness in the past. Their poor drought-stricken neighbors were thankful.

Well, most of them.

One night, two men burst into the hut demanding food and money. "We know you have a box of gold coins," one rough fellow shouted. "Give it to us at once." The men pushed the old woman aside and began to tear the hut apart, searching for the money box.

"Stop!" cried Xiao Sheng in alarm. "I'll give you some money." He pulled the box from its hiding place, but no sooner had he done so than the bigger man grabbed it and opened it.

"What have we here!" he bellowed, holding up the pearl.

Xiao Sheng snatched it from his hand. "You can have all our money, but you can't have the pearl."

The ruffian lunged toward the boy. Quickly Xiao Sheng popped the pearl into his mouth. The man grabbed him by the shoulders and shook him while the other beat upon his back. "Spit it out!" they yelled. "Spit it out or it will be the worse for you!"

Afraid for her son, the old woman began to wail. Poor Xiao Sheng was so confused by all the shaking and shouting that he gulped— and swallowed the pearl!

An intense heat seared through him, as if he had swallowed a ball of fire. He grabbed the teapot and emptied it in one gulp. Then he rushed to the water jar. Ten, twenty, thirty cups he drank, trying to put out the fire. But even after the jar was empty, he craved more water.

His mother and the two men watched helplessly as he rushed outside to the riverbank, threw himself down, and began to drink.

"Stop!" his mother begged.

But he would not and could not stop. Before long, Xiao Sheng had drunk the river dry. And still the pearl burned inside.

The sky darkened and a fierce wind swept along the riverbanks. Lightning crackled. The roar of thunder shook the earth and made it tremble. The villagers clutched one another, gaping at the blackness overhead. Xiao Sheng's mother rushed to his side and clasped him tightly.

"Come inside," she pleaded.

But even as she spoke, a great change was coming over the boy.

Xiao Sheng began to grow— first his legs, then his body. The scales of a fish rippled along his back and the antlers of a deer appeared on his head. His hands became the talons of a hawk and his neck stretched like a snake. As he moved, he felt the twisting and coiling of a serpent's tail, and when he opened his mouth, his mother saw the gleaming pearl.

She stared, amazed. In front of her very eyes, her son had become a dragon!

Xiao Sheng no longer needed to search for wisps of cloud. Throwing back his mighty head, he breathed cloud after cloud and sent them billowing into the sky. As the villagers watched, the clouds burst open and the rain came streaming down. "It's over!" they cried. "Xiao Sheng has ended the drought!" They raised their smiling faces to the life-giving rain and praised the beneficent dragon.

Xiao Sheng sang as the rain poured into the thirsty earth and filled up the river. As he turned toward the river, his mother clung to his legs, trying to hold him back. Gently he freed himself from her grasp. Again and again she flung herself upon him. Again and again he set himself free.

Into the river he went, but his mother's cries pierced his heart and he could not keep from looking back. Each time he turned, his massive body cut into the river's edge, sculpting the banks with his last farewell.

Alone by the river, the mother of Xiao Sheng wept as her son disappeared beneath the surface of the water. And still the rain poured down, washing away her tears.

The villagers were kind to Xiao Sheng's mother and honored her as they honored her son. Each morning they tossed a few grains of rice into the river as a gift to Xiao Sheng, Most Honored and Precious Dragon.

Every evening his mother sat on the riverbank, giving him the news of the day. She told him how the crops flourished and how lush the countryside was, now that the drought was over. She spoke of the strange manner in which the rain fell— how it poured on all the fields except on those of the two wicked men. Those men finally left their dry, barren land in disgrace and were never seen again.

Sometimes a dragonfly landed softly on her shoulder, or a bright orange carp splashed its tail right at her feet. This made her smile, for she knew these to be glimpses of her son. And sometimes when the waters lapped the shore she could hear a light, tinkling sound, as clear and bright as the jingling of golden coins. This, too, made her smile, for she knew she had heard Xiao Sheng singing, "Today is not the same as yesterday."

As long as she lived, she watched for him every spring when dragons rise up from the rivers and breathe clouds to rain upon the earth.

Today in China, the River Min still flows through the province of Szechuan. If you stop by that river to watch sunlight dance upon the water, you will see the banks carved by the dragon's tail.

And if you listen very carefully to the rippling of the water, you may even hear the dragon singing.

A WORD ABOUT DRAGONS

Unlike the fierce fire-breathing dragons of European mythology, Chinese dragons were believed to be water-gods who ascended to the skies each spring to make rain for the benefit of humans. In autumn, they would return to their underwater homes in lakes, pools, rivers, and seas. Since good harvests were so essential to the well-being of the people, it is not surprising that the dragon was worshiped and honored, often at shrines set up in the fields.

Although dragons were always connected with water, their powers went well beyond controlling the tides, creating thunderstorms, breathing clouds, and sending rain. Dragons had the power of transformation. They could become visible or invisible at will, alter their size, or appear as humans, animals, birds, or fish. By controlling the rain, dragons also had the power to protect those who pleased them and punish those who did not.

The dragon was described as having the head of a camel, the horns of a deer, eyes of a rabbit, ears of a cow, neck of a snake, belly of a frog, scales of a carp, claws of a hawk, and soles of a tiger. His voice was like the jingling of copper pans. A pearl was the dragon's most precious possession, which he carefully guarded, keeping it inside his mouth or under his chin. The magic pearl gave off a radiant light that never faded, and had the power to make things multiply.

From the most ancient times in China, the dragon was considered the emblem of royalty and the symbol of greatness. Only the Emperor and his sons were able to use the five-clawed dragon as an ornament on their robes and household effects. A man of great ability or courage was said to be like a dragon. There was no greater honor than to have the dragon's name associated with one's own.